KITTY'S NEW DOLL

By Dorothy M. Kunhardt
Illustrated by Lucinda McQueen

A GOLDEN BOOK • NEW YORK
Western Publishing Company, Inc., Racine, Wisconsin 53404

© 1984 The Estate of Dorothy M. Kunhardt. Illustrations © 1984 Lucinda McQueen. All rights reserved. Printed in the U.S.A. No part of this book may be reproduced or copied in any form without written permission from the publisher. All trademarks are the property of Western Publishing Company, Inc. Library of Congress Catalog Card Number: 92-73289 ISBN: 0-307-30127-3 MCMXCV

Kitty and her mother were going to the toy store.
"You may choose your very own doll," said Mother.
"Choose the one you like best."

At the toy store there were long rows of beautiful dolls.

There was a doll that could close her eyes and say, "Ma-ma."

There was a doll that could wiggle his whiskers and switch his tail.

There was a soldier doll

and a Boy Scout doll

and a nurse doll.

There was a grandmother doll with glasses and a
grandfather doll with a pocket watch.

There was a doll that could really walk and a doll
you could give a bath to.

There was a baby doll that could drink water from a bottle and wet her diaper.

There was an orange doll and a gray doll and a white doll. There was a doll with black fur and white spots.

All the dolls were so wonderful, it was hard for Kitty to choose.

Then, at the end of the row, Kitty saw a rag doll.
The rag doll was made of cloth stuffed with cotton.
Her face was painted on. Her fur was painted on. Her
clothes were painted on. She couldn't do a single
thing, not even sleep.

Kitty thought the rag doll looked as if she were saying, "Choose me. Oh, please, choose me."

Kitty picked up the rag doll and held her in her arms.

"Mother, please, I want this doll," said Kitty.
"Are you sure?" asked Mother. "Wouldn't you rather
have a doll that can close her eyes and go to sleep?

"Or a pretty doll with a long tail just like yours? Do you really want a plain old rag doll that can't do anything at all?"

"She isn't plain," said Kitty. "She can switch her pretend tail and wiggle her pretend whiskers . . .

"and drink from her pretend bottle.

"She can pretend cry and pretend sleep.

"And do you know what I like best of all?" said Kitty.

"What?" asked Mother.

"She can say anything I want her to say," Kitty answered.

"All right," said Mother. "We'll buy her, and she'll
be your very own."

Mother paid for the rag doll.

"Now you're her mother," she said to Kitty.

The two mothers walked home. Kitty hugged her
rag doll. And she pretended the rag doll said, "I love
you, Mother."